The Enchanted Pearl-Away
Kate and Kris have more adventures

Story Ruth Finnegan
Illustrations Sepi

3

THE ENCHANTED PEARL-AWAY

ISBN 978-1-4476-6955-5

YOUNG KATE-PEARL BOOK 4

2023

Callender Press

Old Bletchley

www.callenderpress.co.uk

Prologue
9

Chapter 1 The magic boat
11

Chapter 2 "The Pearl-Away"
24

Chapter 3 Into the real real sea, ahoy
34

Chapter 4 Oh Holly!
46

Chapter 5 In the swirling curling waves
54

Chapter 6 A great storm
62

Chapter 7 Through the fires
74

Chapter 8 In the trees
85

Chapter 9 The Above-The-Clouds-Land
98

Chapter 10 The next adventure
106

THE END
108

Read next
109

NOTES
110

You might like to know
110

The Kate-Pearl series
111

8

Prologue

Two children are dreaming

no dream but the real,

of fear and of courage

of hurricane ventures

 and whales and the sea

and islands and magic

and highways and byways

and finding the hidden

by venturing - where?

                To all that is there,

                    Every day.

So now let us see

let us see…

Chapter 1 The magic boat

"Come on Christopher", said their mum, " you're leaving Kate to do all the work".

" Typical boy, typical boy", said Kate, " Here, you dry these two plates Kris, then I can put them away".

"All right", grumbled Kris. Well, pretended to grumble because he knew Kate was just teasing, and anyway he always loved racing her to see who'd finish their pile of drying-up quicker.

"Thank you both very much", smiled their mum, "you've both been very good. Now you can go and see what your next adventure will be. I wonder".

She waved goodbye but actually she knew very well what it would be like, because she'd had those adventures too when she was a little girl.

She came to the door and flapped the drying cloth after them to say goodbye. Kate waved, Kris just raced on to get to the shore first. He loved it there and he knew Kate would follow. She loved it too.

"Where will they get to this time?" wondered their mum, "will it be the same place as for me or maybe just a little bit different? Older?"

They didn't spare her a thought, or even wonder about their next meal, as they scampered down towards the sea.

Kris and Kate were good friends, cousins. Kris had lived with Kate since his mum had been lost in a great sea storm when he was very little. He didn't really remember her so Kate's mum was really his too, and he was always really happy there (just that there was sometimes *too* much washing up - but that was only after a really special meal).

So - down to the  shore. Holly too. Their darling rascally dog.

When they got there someone was walking by the sea, picking up shells.

They stood and watched him.

"Not sure I like that", said Kris, not unfriendly exactly just - well, not sure what he thought about someone else on what they thought was their *own* bit of shore, up till then they'd always had it to themselves. *Their* shells.

Holly ran back and hid behind a bush at the top of the sand.

But Kate always liked to be friendly. She smiled at the boy.

"I'm Kate", she said,"what's your name?"

"Elik".

"That sounds nice. Does it mean something?"

"I don't know", he said (but I think he did, it was, well, kind of - a bit religious. And *different*).

Kate thought for a bit.

"Maybe something strange - oh I don't know, maybe 'unknown '? 'Roma'? 'divine?' Something special anyway".

" 'Orphan' more like ".

'What!". Kate was *shocked*. "No parents?"

"Well er, I manage", mumbled Elik. "And just look".

He pointed to the little leopard cub that was frisking round his feet, isn't he lovely".

Kate took a hasty step back.

"Does he bite?"

"No never", replied Elik, picking him up and hugging him. The cub licked Elik's cheek.

"You're right", said Kate, "everyone has to have something to love".

But she kept her hands well out of the way. Just in case.

"What's *his* name?" Elik asked, nodding across at Kris who was looking at something in the sand.

" 'Kris'. I think that means someone special. Short for Christopher ".

"Oh", said Elik looking a bit surprised, "well, er, I think he looks quite good and strong, more than me anyway".

"I like your golden skin though", said Kate shyly.

Erik looked embarrassed.

"Some people don't approve of it", he said, "some people say it's best not to mention it, I suppose 'cos it's a bit different from theirs".

"Well, *I* like it", said Kate," it looks so beautiful. And your brown eyes. Did you golden your skin by being outside in the sun a lot?"

"No I don't think so, just born that way I guess".

"Well - ", began Kate.

Kris came running up. "Hi both of you" (he wasn't one to wait for introductions), "I saw a kind of scratching mark, in the sand, it looked like a sail" .

"I know", said Elik, "I saw it too".

"I'm dreaming of going off in a boat of our own", said Kris, "and then we could go to the other side of … ".

"But we haven't *got* a boat". Kate-The-Practical was always down-to-earth. "And I'm certainly not going to swim, can't, I'd be terrified".

"No boat?" said Elik.

"And we've no idea at all how to get one".

 "Of make one", added Kris.

 "Really?" asked Elik, "just look".

He pointed …

"Oh look", cried Kate, "what lovely birds, what are they carrying?"

Elik pointed up again, right above their heads.

Yes, up there in the skies was a flock of birds, a huge crowd, a cloud of them they were so many.

They seemed to be carrying something in their beaks.

"It'll be twigs for their nests", said Kate,

"Just wait", said Elik.

The birds came closer. Then all of a sudden they had dropped the twigs carefully by the very edge of the sea.

The children leaped to catch them.

Look again! The twigs were growing, growing, growing into larger sticks, into branches, into logs, into planks - for a boat!

Look it was growing, bending, curving - fit for a voyage. Magical.

"A catamaran?" said Kate excitedly,

But Kris' father had been a carpenter, and Kris could just remember him even though he'd been gone for years. And Kris knew that *he* would be the skipper, the captain, the One-Who-Knew.

"No Kate, a catamaran has two prows, maybe in your dreams, but for us just one is best (don't look so disappointed Holly, it's not *you* that'll be steering it). A proper boat. One for venturing out in. Even", he took a breath, "even into the real real sea".

Holly must have heard him, because at that moment she came running along the shore with a large large large something - what was it? - in her mouth, running running running down across the sand, awkwardly. It was so long and heavy that she couldn't even run properly, not even walk steadily so the end of it caught Kris and tumbled him into the water. He got up looking cross and shook himself all over them. Holly did too.

So now they were all soaked. But Elik just laughed! (all right for him, the water just ran off him, not like the others). After a while the others did too.

"Well done Holly even though you soaked us", grinned Elik. He looked at the long thing carefully. "It's an *oar*".

"What's that?" asked Kris. "Oh oh, dint tell me, I know - to row with".

"But, but - wouldn't we need *two* oars?" asked Kate.

Holly cocked her ears, then turned round, shaking herself and soaking them again (not Elik, some magic was still keeping him dry!). She raced up the shore and disappeared into the wood.

"Oh dear, has she abandoned you, gone home?" said Elik, pretending to be worried (he knew really that Holly was just like his little leopard - loyal).

"She'd never do that", said Kate and Kris together, "let's just wait".

Sure enough, soon Holly's tail could be seen waving  through the bushes. She was busy with something in there.

"What's happening?" said Kris.

"Sssh", whispered Kate,"look".

Tug tug tug. Holly was pulling at something, she couldn't get it out from the undergrowth but was *not* going to give up.

"Here here Holly, come here, it's all right", called Kris.

She didn't. *Wouldn't.*

Kate raced up the shore to see what it was. Aha. Now she was helping Holly to pull a long long branch that had been tangled up in the brambles.

Tug tug tug.

At last!

Kate and Holly carried it proudly back to the boat.

"The other oar", Kate shouted.

They pulled the boat - the boat!
- down across the sand then
pushed it out into the water till it was just bobbing in the gentle incoming tide.

"Oh *wonderful*", breathed Kate, "she is so beautiful. Precious".

"We did it", said Kris, his eyes alight with joy.

"But we can't row the whole way to the magic island or whatever it is, way off in the sea ...", Kate said, worried.

"Or the skies", said Elik, looking up at the sun, now much further along towards the horizon. Kris followed his glance

"Oh oh!", he shouted, "look at the time, must go".

"It's our teatime", explained Kate,"we'll have to go. Mum …".

They turned to run up the shore, and disappeared into the trees. Elik was left, sitting on the ground, twisting dead seaweed in his hands (what could he be doing?)

But then - a shout. Back came Kris, out of breath.

"The tide's coming in, the tide's coming in, our boar will float away, oh oh what can we do … I'll have to stay to hold her. But oh oh, I *have* to get home for tea. *Now*. And you'd not be strong enough Elik to hold her on your own, and anyway you can't go in the sea, can you".

"Don't worry", said Elik, "don't you see what I'm doing?" - and he held up the seaweed.

But it wasn't seaweed. Not any longer. It was a long thick twisted knotted rope. Strong. One end a coil, the other end free. Snaking across the sand.

"You attach it Kris" , he said.

So Kris waded out with the rope.

"Where?" he called back, for the boat sides were just slippery smooth wood.

"Look at the stern", called Elik.

"Stern? What's that ?" called back Kris. But he was sensible, he started to walk round the boat, And there, at the back, was a chain. With a link. A link that was *just* the right size to put the rope through. And fasten it.

So he did.

He splashed back, water all over Elik yet again. Elik just grinned.

"What now?" said Kris, " I can't stay here all night holding the rope".

"Look", said Elik, pointing up above them.

Sure enough, there was a bird, then the same great flock of birds, even more of them this time.

They came nearer. What were they carrying …

"A stone", said Elik,"to hold your boat safe".

And look - so they were.

A small stone like a bird would carry to its nest. But when they put it down it grew. And *grew*. And *GREW*.

And look it was part of large rock, there all the time buried in the sand. And in the very top of it a jutting upright, just right for the rope.

"Fasten it Kris", said Elik.

So he did.

"Thanks Elik", he shouted as he ran off again, "Teatime. See you tomorrow".

Chapter 2 "The Pearl-Away"

"Thank you children, you were extra quick today", said their mum as she hung up the drying cloths, "I wonder why" (actually looking at their excited faces she had a pretty good idea), "just make sure to be back in time for tea".

"Thanks mum", said Kate,

"Thanks mum", said Kris.

Off they raced. Holly was asleep in the sun, like dogs do, but she always knew when there was an adventure on and raced after them, her tail flying in the air after her.

And there was the boat, bobbing in the water, tied firmly to the jutting rock. Elik was watching her happily and the little leopard was leaping round him, jumping over and under the rope to show how clever he was.

"She's so beautiful", whispered Kate, looking at the boat, "do you think she has a, a name?"

"Woof", said Holly.

She looked *very* affronted when Kris laughed at her, so Kate patted her comfortingly.

"Never mind, Holly, I thing 'woo-' , ah, 'Wood' would be a lovely name for a wooden boat".

"Not wooden", said Kris firmly,"*magical.* She'll fly to the ends of the world and back. Anyway dogs don't name ships".

"I suppose you think *you* do then Kris? Huh!"

"Well why not, do *you* have any ideas?"

"No", admitted Kate,"I don't. Anyway maybe we don't need to bother with a name for her anyway, it's nice just looking at her, seeing how beautiful she is, like a pearl on the sea, so so lovely".

They looked at her together. Even Holly perked up her tail and gave a little wuff.

"That's it', said Kris suddenly.

"What's it?" asked Kate.

"Her name - 'Pearl', exactly right".

"Mm yes, 'Pearl', and -

" 'Pearl *Away*", interrupted Kris, "I'm going away in her. Round the world".

His eyes looked far away. Imagining it. His dream.

"I'm coming too", insisted Kate.

"If you dare, you're only a - ".

"So long as Holly comes too".

They looked at each other and nodded. Holly nodded too, a dog-nod. And WiseOwl flew down onto Kate's shoulder and nodded *her* head as well.

"Let's go then", said Kris, striding off towards the boat, "Come on Holly" (he didn't need to say "Come on Kate", he knew she was right behind him).

But then Kate stopped, uncertain.

"Are we *really* going to go away all round the world Kris?" Kate asked, "I'd like that but I really don't want to row all that way, I'd be exhausted and we'd never be home in time for tea".

"Mm", said Kris, "yes difficult. I don't - Oh come back Holly, we can't have you scampering off just when we're going".

Holly took no notice. She had her own ideas. She was looking up at the sky.

They all looked, Elik and his little leopard and WiseOwl too.

The wind was puffing along past them, blowing up the sand, ruffling Holly's ears, whistling through the bushes, rustling up the wavelets.

What was it?

"Oh oh, the North Wind", exclaimed Kate suddenly, "I can feel him. Coming closer".

The little leopard squeaked in panic and ran to hide behind Elik.

"It's all right little Leo-kin", said Kate "he's coming to help us, to blow us out across the sea".

"Not much use trying to blow a wooden boat and a bare mast", said Kris sulkily.

But Holly was still at work. She raced up the sand and came back with the jacket that Kate had thrown down on the ground (not folded or hung up as it should have been her mum would've said). She brought it to Kate and put it on the ground in front of her, then sat there looking expectantly at Kate.

"Er, what?" wondered Kate.

WiseOwl was still on Kate's shoulder and whispered something in her ear.

"Oh", said Kate, and pulled a crumpled handkerchief out of the left jacket pocket.

It started to grow and grow and grow as they watched. What was it?

Suddenly - "It's a sail", they all shouted.

The swallows came again and dropped small twigs that became long straight spars to connect the spreading sail to the mast, and S-Snake, the snake in Elik's hands, twisted itself into ropes to control the sail.

"*Halyards* they're called", said Kris (how did he know? Perhaps he was magic too in those magical far-off fairytale times?)

The mast was now standing upright, high, in the boat, and the sail filled out in the wind. The sails. .

"Magic", whispered Kate to herself, "Miracle".

"No magic", whispered WiseOwl back, "it's created by you. Your insight, your imaginati-on".

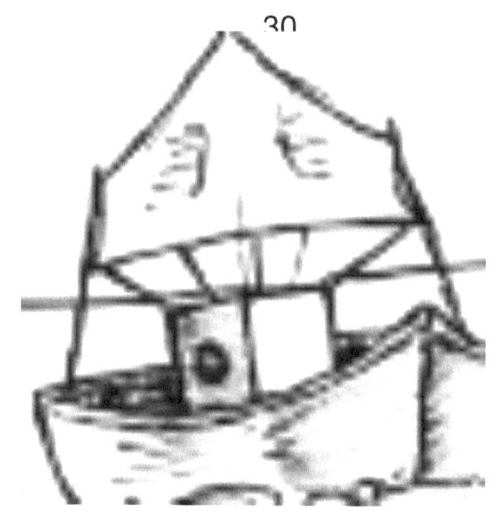

Anyhow, there she was, the Pearl-Away.

She was so so beautiful.

Ready to go.

And Kate and Kris, and behind them Holly ("Wait for me, wait for me, bark bark"), all climbed carefully into the boat.

Their Pearl-Away. Longing to go.

Elik waved them goodbye.

He was staying on land. His little tame leopard cub didn't like water. And nor did he.

"Goodbyeee …".

So now Kris and Kate were *really* sailing, right into the deep ocean.

"I was sorry to say goodbye to our friend Elik", said Kris.

"Me too", said Kate".

"Woof", said Holly.

"I kind of feel a bit alone, he sort of protected us".

"Wohh! *Not*" grunted Holly, thinking of Elik's little leopard (a cat!), she thoroughly disagreed, *thoroughly*. It was *good* to leave them behind.

"Maybe we'll meet someone else out here? Someone new?"

"Ye-es", said Kate, thinking hard,"My mam did once tell us something about … ".

"A witch", said Kris, "but aren't witches bad?"

"Not this one, I think she said, yes, um, yet, Heloful-Witch-of-the-Seas. I think she helps if we're stuck in a dead calm or …"

"Or a dreadful, killing, blinding, winding storm. Yes, maybe. Hope we don't need her" (but secretly I think that he did, don't you, he liked adventures so he could be brave and skilful and learn a lot. Just so long as Kate was all right and they were home in time for tea).

"But how do we call her, is there a special spell?"

"Maybe she just comes", said Kate, "we'll see".

But what came was a mighty mighty frightening eagle.

It made straight for Kate.

It broke the rope - "Oh, the halyard", said Kate, but that didn't help her. The eagle started to pull her up off the ship.

" No no no", she shouted. Panic.

"Jump jump", shouted Kris.

"No, don't cling on. *Jump*".

She did. Straight into the sea.

The eagle laughed and flew off. It was only wanting a game.

Kate was struggling, she *could* sort-of swim but wasn't very good at it at all, well actually to tell the truth she couldn't really, and oh dear, the silly girl, she'd forgotten to put on her life-jacket. Panic again.

Would Kris turn the boat back for her?

Yes, yes, oh yes, he was coming ...

But -

Oh no no no, look out! A flock of blue clashing rocks are coming fast, faster, faster, straight at her, about to -

No!!!

If only she was at home, safe with her mam. It only this was just a dream.

Was it do you think?

Chapter 3 Into the real real sea, ahoy

"Time to get up lazy bones". It was her mum's voice. "Kris has already finished his breakfast and is raring to go. Wake up!".

Kate leapt out of bed.

"Oh oh, it was a dream, oh thank goodness. No eagle after all, no drowning in the sea without a life-belt".

Her mum smiled. "Yes we all have bad dreams sometimes", she said, "never mind, you're safe now. Hungry?"

"Yes oh yes, *very*. Thank you mum".

"Eat up then, Kris is waiting for you".

She didn't spend long, did she, even though she was so very hungry (who wouldn't be after all these adventures, even if they weren't quite real - but they *were*, Kate knew it).

The two children were in such a hurry to get back to their Pearl-Away that they forgot all about the washing-up. Even to say goodbye, what wretches.

But their mum just smiled and waved. She knew what it was like.

Holly was torn, she thought she should stay with their mother since they hadn't bothered to say goodbye - just to show that *she* was loving and polite. Also she knew she'd got them into trouble lots at times and didn't want *that* to happen again.

But their mum just laughed and said "It's all right Holly, off you go. I think this time *you* are going to be the one that saves them, so goodbye for now, see you later, your bone'll be waiting when you get back, don't worry".

So off Holly rushed after them.

Their mum smiled. "Yes, they're safe at home. But safety isn't everything, kids want adventure too, I know. They *need* it. Dogs too I think".

It was true. Holly had rushed after them so fast that she was before them on the shore. There she was, trying to make friends with the little leopard - not easy for a dog, you know, with a, well, with a kind of *cat* - but there they were frisking together. Elik was still keeping a careful eye on them.

But now - look look, magic - they were all on the boat together, Kate and Kris, and Holly (*she* was looking nervously over the side).

And now the sail was up, it really was a magical boat and they were sailing in the deep ocean with the wind whistling through the ropes.

"Halyards you mean", said Kris.

"Same difference", said Kate cheekily (why not be cheeky when she was, oh, so so cheerful and happy, just sitting there hearing the wind in the ro- , er, in the sails).

Kris was holding the tiller, steering, being the captain, the skipper, The-One-Who-Knows, he thought a boy should do that, anyway he was older (only a few days, but still …). Calmly.

Kate was managing the sails, he couldn't do without *that*. She had her life-jacket on. *This* time.

"Sails are the *important* thing", she said to Holly, "delicate, subtle, making us go or stop. *Steering's* easy, we're in the middle of the sea, nothing to bang into, it's we girls need to take charge and look out".

Holly wagged her tail. She agreed, she was a girl too you know.

They sailed on and on, Under the sky, the clouds the sun. Skimming like a bird. Like flying.

It was wonderful.

Can it last for ever? thought Kate.

What was that? Voices? A song?

A song! in the middle of the sea? Impossible.

Kate at the sail, and Kris at the tiller listened, entranced.

Part of their wonderful dream, Fantastic. *Music* too!

Holly was at the prow, eager to continue their magical voyage. She listened for a moment, ears perked up, pricked.

Then her ears dropped. She snuffed the air and made a nasty face (yes, dogs can you know). She seemed to be saying

"There's something bad out there. I'm not coming".

She sniffed. It was a nasty smell, horrid. She turned her back to the front of the boat, showing she wanted to go the other way, *away* from where they were going, *away* from where the smell was.

"Oh Holly", said Kris and Kate together, "the singing is beautiful, and it's a lovely song. Lovely words. *Listen*".

They did.

> *Life is short, but life is sweet;*
> *and even men of brass and fire must die.*
> *The brass must rust, the fire must cool,*
> *for time gnaws all things in their turn.*
> *Life is short, but life is sweet.*

"Let's get closer", said Kris.

"Ye-es, perhaps", said Kate who felt she heard WiseOwl whispering in her ear. But she still held onto the sail, they were still sailing nearer and nearer and the sun was streaming down on them with its golden rays, like long locks of hair, half blinding them.

Nearer and nearer.

Holly couldn't bear it. She *knew* they were sailing into dreadful dreadful danger.

She leaped onto Kate, who was holding the sail ropes, and what did she do? She bit at Kate's wrist, yes *bit*. Holly would never never bite Kate, she only did it to show this was something really really important. To try to save them.

Kate let out a yell, no, a *shriek*. Not that it was painful, just it wasn't what you would expect from Holly. She was so shocked that she completely let go of the rope. The sail started to tumble down and the ship slowed.

But Kris the skipper still held steady on the tiller. He was steering straight straight straight towards the sound of the voices, his eyes were entranced as he listened.

Holly knew he'd not be deterred by a mere bite, so she *hurled* herself at Kris and knocked his hand off the tiller. The ship turned round and came to a stop deep in the trough of a great wave. They saw the next wave curling over them, coming and coming and coming down at them to send the ship to the bottom.

But Holly was too quick for it. She leaned with all her weight on the tiller, and there they were sweeping up over the next wave, there they were, safe on its top, steering away from the voices.

They were safe, sailing on again, safe on the dark deep blue sea under the blue blue sky. All was quiet, just a gentle wind following them and helping them on and Kris again holding the tiller.

"Oh thank you Holly', said Kate, "that was close".

"Thank you Holly", said Kris the skipper, The-One-Who-Knows, "what a good thing you were with us".

"Woof" said Holly, looking as if they'd be needing her again. Proud of herself!

"We were so lucky", said Kate "I remember now that mum once told us that those voices sounded so beautiful that they lured many many sailors to their death".

"Nearly us", admitted Kris.

So on they sailed, contented, across the deep blue sea.

And under the blue blue sky.

They saw many monsters as they sailed through the waves. But Kris steered the boat fast through them. And when the seaweed clung to the bottom of the boat he reached down and pulled them free.

And Kate admired him from where she sat holding the halyards amidships, and Holly stood proud on the prow. They were all working together, one fine team.

So then they came to the wandering blue rocks, those Kate had dreamed of once.

They saw them in the distance coming fast toward them, they saw them shining like spires and castles and turrets of bright glass, while an ice-cold wind blew from the north and filled the sails and chilled their hearts. Even Holly's.

And they neared them. Heaving rocks rolling on the long sea-waves, crashing and grinding together. The sea sprang up in spouts between them, and swept round them in white sheets of foam. The rocks towered high in air above them and the wind whistled over their heads, terrifying them.

Oh! And it was a *good* thing now that Kris was at the tiller. He nodded to Kate to pull down the sail.

"Loosen halyards", he ordered, "and be brave" (he looked at Holly, he knew *Kate* was always brave), and searched for a way to get through.

"Double double bubble ho", sang Kate as loud as she could - the witch's spell her mother had sung to her once, she couldn't remember it all but maybe a little bit would be enough.

"We have to squeeze between those two rocks that are rushing towards us", yelled Kris as loud as he could, trying to be heard over the clatter of the rocks, "or else - ".

He didn't say what else. But Kate knew. Too well.

She held her breath.

Still rushing towards them.

Oh oh.

Still rushing …

Rushing.

Faster faster faster,

"Oh oh mam", cried Kate. What else could she do?

Holly didn't think, not even of the bone waiting for her at home. She leaped on the prow, she made herself as big as big as *huge* as she could, huge like a cloud in the sky and wide as the horizons (nearly) and as strong and as weighty-heavy-round as the earth.

So when the rocks rushed on them she was too big for them, she pushed and wedged them apart. The boat *just* squeezed through.

Then the rocks clashed together with a fine bang, the toppest crags of them, clanging, lastest. And they had caught - oh caught - *the tip of Holly's tail*. That's the reason, dear children, that Holly and all the dogs like her have only half a tail. One side proud, whirling, upright. the other - well, *nothing.* Or maybe that's only magic dogs.

Anyhow, look, just a little white tip from Holly's tail left clinging to the rocks. And it's still there, a flag warning mariners of the peril, to save many lives.

And so - they were *through*. Kate and Kris, and Holly (shorter tail) on the prow.

And listen - here she is rejoicing and barking and crying out in her doggie way.

"We're through, bow, bow wow wow. Due to *me*, bow wow".

So on they sailed, into the deep, the unknown.

Afraid but not afraid.

And above them flew the flock of magic birds. Spirits. Watching, guarding them across the sea.

And bringing them home - ready for the next adventure.

Chapter 4 Oh Holly!

Kris and Kate and Holly sailed on into the deep blue sea. What a lovely boat. And beautiful fish to watch.

It was early on the next day and so so peaceful. A gentle wind was blowing the boat along. Kris at the tiller thought it was wonderful.

The waves slowly got a little higher, and started to show white crests.

"Time to turn back", said Kate firmly.

"Well - okay", said skipper Kris, "if you know how! In these waves?"

Kate tried hard not to cry. She stumbled out with:

"Well, well then I guess we'll just have to go through with it. But you *will* turn us won't you when the wind dies down, it has to, it has to".

"Yes of course Kate. We're all in the same boat you know, haha".

"Well I'll pray, *much* more useful than your silly jokes".

Holly looked unimpressed. *She* would show them. Some day. Some *other* day.

The waves rose a bit higher. Not very high, you know, but enough to really frighten Kate. "Oh this is so awful", she whispered to herself,"I'm really afraid only I mustn't let anyone know. Specially Holly".

(Actually I think Holly *did* know, don't you. Dogs do. She snuggled closer to Kate, comfortingly).

"Oh mam, how I wish you were here! Oh oh oh".

Then she sat up straighter, Kate-The-Practical. "But anyway I have Holly. I'll look after *her*, whatever. I'm no good at steering so I'll just have to be the grown-up brave girl you tell me I am, mam. *Sensible*".

She gulped, she didn't really feel very sensible *or* practical inside, but still - And maybe the sea wasn't really so rough after all when she looked at it. When she was being sensible, being Kate-The-Practical.

And Holly looked as if she was loving it, so it *must* be all right.

What was Holly looking at over the side, wagging her tail, a little bark?

Ah, a shoal of darting colourful wriggling fish. Kate gasped as she saw Holly riveted by them, then, oh no!, getting ready to jump at them.

"No no no Holly, they're not rats, no no no, not for chasing". She clutched desperately at Holly.

Too late. Holly had wriggled out of her grasp, and, leapt into the sea.

She disappeared in the waves.

"Oh Kris Kris, stop - Holly!"

But the wind blew on and the boat couldn't stop. It swept rapidly on, Holly was left behind.

Oh oh worse, Kris had gone in after Holly oh so brave so wonderful to go after Holly.

But - now he was gone too. Kate was left behind, alone. And if even Kris hadn't been able to turn the boat, how could she?

It was plunging and bucking and galloping and getting further and further and further away from where she'd last seen Kris and Holly.

And the waves were getting higher and the wind was whistling round and she couldn't go back.

She was useless.

And alone.

And terrified.

She could just get glimpses of Kris's head in the waves,

and Holly's.
They were left behind. Getting smaller all the time. Further and further away.

She heard a faint faint cry, Kris 's voice.

"The boat Kate. Bring it back".

But Kate had no idea how. All she could do was watch Holly's half-tail, white, and Kris's head getting smaller and smaller in the distance. And smaller again.

Now she was alone in the ocean. All she could do was pray. Or try to remember that spell for the SeaWitch.

She shut her eyes to do it.

Something suddenly made them open, a slight tug somewhere near her feet.

She looked down. Something was moving.

It was a rope spinning out from a coil on the deck, nearly at an end, unwinding, unwinding, now only the tiniest bit was left - around and around, unwinding.

Kate leapt on it and ju-ust managed to catch the very end before it was all gone. With a long hard struggle she snatched it and looped it round the mast and tied it fast.

She wondered what next.

Then it was as if SeaWitch's voice was telling her.

"PULL, Kate, PULL. Pull on the rope".

Oh it was hard! She grunted and moaned with the effort and the pain. She was exhausted. But she was *not* going to give up. Never.

Suddenly she felt an extra weight on the rope.

"It's him it's him, oh it must be, oh Kris!"

She tried even harder, nearly fainting from exhaustion.

Gradually, something appeared in the sea.

Kris's head.

Then Holly's.

With an almighty effort, Kate hauled them on board. Kris was fastened to the end of the rope, and he had a fast hold of Holly's collar.

Kris pointed to the rope fastened to his life-jacket. "Told you we should put them on and fasten the rope, I just knew they'd save us one day".

He grinned cheekily at Kate. Kate smiled back, specially when he sat down abruptly on a bollard. *He* was exhausted too (no wonder). But still grinning.

Holly just wagged her tail triumphantly and lay down with a small fish in her mouth - for her that was of course the whole point of the very satisfactory episode!

"Oh Holly!" exclaimed Kate and Kris, not able to stop themselves laughing from relief.

"Oh Holly!" came an echo - was it Elik who loved them from across the sea?

"So my praying was good, Kris", said Kate. "That was what saved us".

"You're right Kate", whispered skipper Kris. "In the end *you* were the strong one. Wise".

On the shore Elik nodded, with smile, and WiseOwl sent a soft hoot through the trees.

"Yes", agreed Kate, "but next time I'll keep a tighter hold on Holly".

"Yes", agreed her mum, "teatime".

Chapter 5 In the swirling curling waves

Next morning Kris and Kate and Holly were back down on the shore early. Eager to go. Elik and Little Leopard waved them off, WiseOwl hooted for them, and the birds guided them from above.

What adventures they were having! They were sailing through the sea again, Kris and Kate and brave Holly. A light breeze, Kris-The-Skipper,

The-One-Who-Knows, the great sailor, at the helm, Kate dabbling her toes in the water.

So all was well.

Further they ventured, then further still. On again through the dark water and the moonlit starry nights. A long way round the world - that was Kris's dream. So all indeed was well.

"Hold on Kate", said Kris warningly, "I'm about to tack".

"Tack?" said Kate sleepily, "do the sails need mending then? Darning?"

"Don't be silly", said Kris the skipper, "it's when you make the boat zigzag back and forwards to get the best of the wind".

"Oh", said Kate even more sleepily. "I'll just snuggle up to Holly then, I feel so sleepy, I'll just shut my eyes for a moment".

So she did, and let go her hold, and on they sailed.

All was quiet, peaceful. The sun was rising, red and gold, a small flock of birds above keeping pace with them.

"Watch out Kate", called Kris sharply and swung the boat round.

He looked across. Where was Kate? No Holly either.

And oh oh, there was Kate, struggling in the water. Holly was peeping over the side at her, half out of the boat, very worried but *not* about to jump in after her.

No, *not*.

And Kate? She opened her eyes. Just sea around her, sky above, boat going away, away, away from her. Why don't they turn back? What can Kris do? or Holly?

Ah, she was adrift. Kate. Alone.

Oh oh, not alone, all those scary creatures.

But yes, in herself, alone. Very alone.

Baked in the sun, dried in the wind, parching in thirstiness. Struggling to keep afloat.

But now, oh oh, *sinking.*

She opened her eyes. Yes it was just like her mum had told her, there were all those "fascinating creatures of the deep".

Well, maybe they were fascinating. But not now, Not for her.

Surface again.

No better. Just the waves, the sky, the sun the sun the sun. Burning.

They had forgotten her. Sailed on. Away. Even Holly, dear Holly, even Holly.

Was that a bark across the sea? No just a seagull calling.

Horrible seagulls.

Kate closed her eyes. Might as well die now.

Oh then a head in water. Kris? *Kris*!

Coming towards her. Swimming. Came beside her.

"Hold on to me Kate", she thought she heard him say, "You'll be all right now".

But -

"Not all right", gulped Kate, mouth full of water, "The boat" , gulp, "the boat. No boat. Gone".

"We'll get her", said Kris, "Our lovely Pearl-Away".

"I can't swim all the way round the world for her", cried Kate, grumpily, gulpily, "I'm exhausted already, can't you see, I just want to go back to sleep. And oh oh, where's Holly", she was screaming now, "*Holly*".

"Don't worry", said Kris again, "Look".

She looked. No boat. Just sky. Sun glaring, burning.

Ship still sailing away. No ship.. Sky, sun above, "Kris, look, boat gone, we're lost".

Ah, what's this?

A long rope is snaking through the sea, under the sea, over the sea. Again?

Made by Elik? Long ago. Ready to save them. Magical.

Tied to Kris.

And now Kris is pulling on the rope, nearing them to the boat, go on, go on, Kris, on …

Oh oh and now, so strange, she felt Kris and Holly looking at her. Close.

Kate shut her eyes in relief. She was saved!

The next thing she knew was -

Ahh, soft touch on her cheek, moisture, wetness she never thought to feel again.

Holly's moist tongue was licking her. There where she was, lying on the deck, waking up. From her dream. Aah.

Lovely sea gulls in the sky.

Kris was at the helm and looking up, skipper eyes narrowed, at the clear blue sky.

"It'll be an easy ride today I think", he said.

"Yes", said Kate, pulling up the sails.

Holly, proud, up front, wagged what was left of her tail, white.

But the sun was setting. Oh oh oh, they were *late*, they would miss their tea.

"Double double toil and trouble". Kate had suddenly remembered more of the spell.

And - it worked!

They felt themselves lifted up like in a magic carpet -

it was surely the SeaWitch - Kate and Kris and Holly and the ship - and carried across the sea, a flock of birds flying around them making comforting sounds. Singing, as birds do. Magic.

And - there they were on the shore, the Pearl-Away, intact and undamaged, no sign of the Sea-Witch, just a small wisp of cloud drifting away in the clouds.

Oh and there was Elik, watching them with a smile, and his little leopard playing with the waves at the edge of the sea, running away whenever they came anywhere near him - he thought he was *so* brave and clever "chasing them away"!

WiseOwl was perched on the mast, looking at them approvingly.

"Well done", she said, "you're back in time for tea".

"Yes, and I'm *so* hungry", said Kris and raced up the shore.

"Me too", said Kate, but she waited a moment to call thank you after the wispy cloud and smile at WiseOwl and Elik. Then off she ran home, Holly dancing after her.

"We're back mum", she shouted.

Chapter 6 A great storm

So on they were sailing across the deep sea, Kris and Kate and too-brave Holly. Lost. But maybe not wholly lost, for the birds watched over them.

And their mother.

She had looked up at the sky, it was beautiful and sunny. The children would be all right. And Holly.

But - look there on the west: a small cloud, smaller than a man's hand, climbing, rapid, bigger and bigger and bigger and *bigger.*

"A storm on the way", said mum, "it's coming their way, fast. I think they will come through, at least they remembered their life-jackets, I only hope they've put them on and *fastened* them, Holly will take care too and look after them".

She knew a storm could kill them like it had many people, but she told herself not to worry. Holly was there. And the SeaWitch. And the birds.

Even so she sent up a wee prayer for them.

All this time the boat - it was a proper *ship* by now (well it needed to be, it was in the real sea) - the ship was sailing across the smooth ocean way, no waves, just a little rustle-ruffle-wrinkle on the top of the water.

"I think we should be back in time for tea", said Kate.

"Wuff", said Holly.

"Yes all right, and for your bone Holly", smiled Kate.

But - but now the sails are flapping in the Wind-No-Wind.

"What can we do?", shouted Kate,"we've stopped. In the middle of the sea. Stymied-stopped-stuck".

Kris looked round. "Silly! have you never heard of oars?"

So Kris and Kate shouted, and Holly barked, and all three manned the oars (well Holly dogged them, pushing and pulling with her paws and her tail - not the best way you'll say, but there you are, we all love dogs).

So they all were rowing now. *Got away.* The oars bent beneath their strokes as they swept through the sea.

If only the wind would get up again they were

thinking.

Well - *it did.* For the Sea-Witch had heard their wish (Kris and Kris didn't know yet to be careful what they wished for (you too!)). *Holly* knew but they didn't listen to her (and anyway she didn't always remember her own good advice).

So they sail-ed on, all safe again, in the fine breeze they'd wished for. And all seemed peaceful and well as they continued on through the lightly tossing sea in Pearl-Away, their magic boat.

Now the wind was whistling round them. But they were not really afraid because they'd had a good breakfast before setting out and they knew their mum was thinking about them.

But -

But - Holly was listening.

What was it? A whistle? The kind of high high whistling only dogs can hear?

Holly tried to warn them, bark bark bark.

"It's all right Holly", said Kate, bending down to stroke her, "We'll soon be on our way home for tea - oh and for your bone, don't worry".

But Holly did worry, she pawed at Kate, jumped up, nearly toppled into the sea.

"Holly, behave", said Kris. When he was the skipper he could be quite firm, "*Sit!*".

Holly sat, trembling. She wasn't afraid of Kris, just of what she knew was c-coming. Fast. Kate put her arms round her.

"Quiet Holly, I'm here", she whispered,

The whistling became louder and louder and louder. Then louder still.

The boat began to rock.

And rock.

And rock.

The clouds were gathering,

stirring up from the sea the rage of every

wind on earth.

The sea and sky were hidden in cloud. And it became blacker than night.

Winds from East, South, North, and West fell upon them, all at the same time, and a tremendous sea got up.

And it broke over the Pearl-Away with such terrific fury that she reeled again and again and again, and even Kris-The-Skipper, the strong one, had to let go the helm.

The winds were so hard and fierce that they broke the mast half way up, and half of the sail went over into the sea and the ship was covered with water and disappeared in the spray.

Oh oh, disaster!

And then, look, her mast was appearing through the surf, then her deck - but oh tossed all about. Think how the winds of autumn whirl dry leaves round and round on a road. Yes, like that. The winds were playing ball games with the ship, back and forwards between them. For hours on end.

Then a *terrible great wave* reared itself up up and up, and more up as Kate held her breath (a*nd all the world too I think - up, up, UP ...*) above their heads, till it *broke.* It burst right over them and the ship shuddered like a heap of dust blown all about by a whirlwind.

This must be the end for them all three.

Kate clung on to Holly with one hand, the snake-rope that Elik had twisted round the mast - now just the stump of a mast - with the other. Kris the brave skipper, eyes half shut against the wind, looking into the waves ahead, struggled back and clung fast to the tiller. He'd found it again, brave Skipper Kris, and fixed it firm to its place.

The wind caught the remnant of the sail with a shriek and it fell right down on top of them.

No way could Kris steer. Where where would they end up?

"Oh oh look Kris!" cried Kate suddenly, "Land! We're saved. Land ahoy, land ahoy, land - ".

"Stupid girl", shouted Kris rudely, "don't you know that in a storm the greatest danger is land. Specially great high cliffs, just look! Safest place is out at sea".

"Oh", said Kate,"I didn't know".

"Wuff", said Holly (it wasn't clear which of them she was agreeing with).

The horizon was now blacked out, no longer any birds to be seen. CRASHES from the waves.

Kris was wrestling with the tiller. But, oh, they were drifting closer and closer to those fearsome frightening jagging rocks.

Kris was right. What more dangerous for ships, small, large, even magic ones, than jagged rocky reef-y land. And look, all around the shore lay broken ships ...

Kris could no longer control the ship. He just left to tiller to steer itself. All he could do was just let the winds blow them to - well, to anywhere.

No no! The white surging surf was thundering up and up against the rocks and the waves burst against them all the more, and everything was covered in spitting splitting surging suffocating spray.

There was no harbour there for a ship to stay, no shelter. Just jutting headlands and rocks and rocks and rocks. And the wind driving them right right right onto them. Fast. Then faster. Nothing they could do.

The waves reached to the horizons - hashing, lashing, dashing, crashing, boiling, curling above and below and between. Everywhere.

CRASH.

Great stones around, above, below.

Boat all right?

Yes, for one instant. But -

But then a great wave lifted her high high high above their heads and SMASHED her down.

And Kris and Kate with her. Holly too.

So now just million smithereen-shards,

Ship broken, tiller wrenched from the skipper's hand, Kris, Kate, Holly stunned, bruised, winded, broken, flung onto the jagged tearing hard-pain rocks.

Kris picked himself up. Looked round. The tiller lay broken in three pieces. The mast disappeared. And the ship in a million splintered bits.

Smashed to - to worse than smithereens.

Beyond repair.

No way home now.

Holly began to howl, holding up a sore paw. Kate managed to pull herself up and climbed over to hug Holly.

"It's all right, it's all right Holly, we'll look after you, poor paw, never mind it's all right" (she knew it *wasn't* all right but it always helped to have Holly to look after ("Good girl", she felt her mum say)).

"It's *not* all right", shouted Kris furiously. "Just look!"

He held up the broken tiller, he pointed to the broken ship. The pieces.

"Oh my own my own, my ship, dear Pearl-Away, never to sail again, oh my life, nevermore to fly through the free air of the sea, under the sails, under the moon and stars ... ".

Kris never cried, but this time he burst into tears.

Tears of anger? Yes. But more - despair, a life end.

"Can we mend her?" asked Kate-The-Practical coming over to help. He threw her off in fury. Real furiously (that wasn't really like Kris - but he was in shock. No wonder).

Holly dogged quick out of his way. More sensible than Kate.

"Now we're here, let's explore", said Kate making the best of it, "it looks like a beautiful island once we get across these rocks. Trees, and grass and ... And maybe there'll be a king who'll help us and teach us wisdom. WiseOwl once told me … ".

Kris didn't hear her, he was looking at his broken ship, tears in his eyes.

"Oh Pearl-Away, Pearl-Away, my dearest Pearl-Away, I've wrecked you, you'll never sail again, and I can't … "

"Well, that's why we need to explore, get help", said Kate-The-Practical, "someone who can mend her".

"*Mend* her! When she's lying there in a million splinters! No one, no one can mend her".

"Oh if only we were home mam", whispered Kate, hugging Holly.

And suddenly she felt they were all there, even Holly; just putting away the clean dry dishes.

Had it all been a bad dream (well, not *all* bad)?

"I was thinking of you", said their mother, "and so were Elik and WiseOwl. We knew you'd be all right in the end if we kept thinking about you, and that if you looked after Holly you'd be safe back home in time to help with the washing up".

So just a dream?

"Teatime", said their mother, putting the pancakes on the table.

"*What* an exciting day you've had".

It was, wasn't it!

Chapter 7 Through the fires

Kate and Kris carefully put away the breakfast things and hung up the drying cloths. For once they'd been quick.

"Thank you children", said their mum. "Have a good day".

"Race you to the boat", shouted Kris and dashed off.

He was soon there, jumping over a small pile of ashes at the edge of the trees, giving them a quick kick as he went.

"Hurry up Kate", he shouted, "Now for our next adventure".

Holly was quick after him. She didn't bother to jump, just ran quickly through, leaving ashes flying in the air behind her.

Kate had stopped for a minute to give her mum a quick kiss, then raced after him. She was usually a faster runner than Kris but this time he'd got too good a start for her to catch him.

As she got nearer the shore she'd nearly caught him. She'd seen him in front, lightly jumping over a small pile in the bushes at the edge of the sand.

"No problem", she thought, and raced hard after, longing to reach the Pearl-Away, their magic boat, and get going on their next adventure.

But -

In the short time it had taken her to reach the edge of the woods and look down on the shore *something had happened.*

Something Very Frightening.

When Kris had jumped over the ashes he didn't know they were still warm.

"No no", WiseOwl had said in his ear, "go back and stamp out the heat or it'll flare up, and then …".

But Kris had just seen his beautiful ship, there, waiting for him. Longing to go.

So he didn't listen.

He just rushed down onto the sand, not looking back. Holly too.

But there, behind them?

A flicker, a tiny flame, a flare, another flame, a burning fiery blaze - a FIRE.

Up into two trees it swept, alive, aflame, a-high up to the sky.

Kate came. Running,

What she saw was - a *wall* of flame, A forest fire in front of her.

Oh no! She'd always been afraid of fire (quite right!).

She had to get through, she had to get through, to Kris, he'd be waiting for her. And the Pearl-Away too, ready to go.

But she was afraid.

 Kate turned right round and raced back to her mam.

"Mam mam what can I do? I must must get to the boat, I must get to Kris, he's waiting for me, Holly too".

"Go on then, washing up finished".

"But but but - the fire…".

"Oh? Well, all you need to do is take some deep breaths, go back, then just go round to one side or other of the flames. Right or left, doesn't matter which. Easy. Then you can get round, then straight down to the sea. Okay?"

"Yes", said Kate in a small voice. "won't you come too?"

"No", said her mam. She knew it was best for Kate to do it *herself*.

"Please".

Kate was always quite brave, but - fire!

"All right, I'll try", she said. Brave Kate! Still frightened.

She went back to the flaming fire of trees, it was even brighter and bigger by now, a real forest fire.

She *tried*.

She went to the left. No way past, just the end of the shore, then cliff.

She went to the right. No way past there either, just high rocks, too steep to climb. Too hot too.

"Oh Kris", she cried, "help me, I'm sorry I ran away, the fire was less then, I *could* have got round to you *then* but I was a coward. If only … If only you would come to help. But … too late".

Surely, she thought, she was clever enough, wasn't she? She could surely find a way to get round?

"Go round wide", she told herself, it's only a bonfire.

She tried again to the right.

But it had extended itself, wider and wider, starting to race back towards her, to encircle her. Ohh!

Now it was a burning, flaming, bursting, *raging* forest fire, right across the shore, the world, Kris on the other side.

She tried to go *through* it.

Too hot hot hot, too fiery, flaming, fearsome, Frightening. She was afraid of it.

She shut her eyes in despair.

Ah, what was that through the flames, through the smoke. Answering her imagination, imagining.

A fire engine. A full fire crew. And Holly sitting next the driver, very proud (I think she thought that she was driving it - typical! dear Holly). It came out, it stopped next to her.

Oh oh saved", cried Kate in her dream, "you can take me through. To Kr- ".

"Only volunteer firemen allowed on board miss", said the driver, not friendlily, not friendlily at all. He turned the truck ready to drive back through the fire, the way he'd come.

'That's all right", shouted Kate above the fierce crackle of the flames, "I'd like to be a volunteer fireman and help fight fires, help people, help the woods, the world. Go with you to the edge of the sea".

"Girls not allowed", he said gruffly and swung the wheel.

"But but why not, why not?" asked Kate, outraged (quite right too, girls just as good as boys at - well, at anything … specially if it's Kate).

"Because, because .., er because ..". He stopped to think, "oh just because - Stop arguing, it's er, obvious".

Grinding of gears, cross-sounding, disappearing into the smoke.

Kate was alone. Even Holly gone.

But she was not going to be beaten.

Kate wanted to cry but she knew she mustn't. So she sat down instead and she thought and thought.

"I can't go through, and I can't go round, then - "

She'd no idea (you know what's that's like, don't you).

Then suddenly a thought struck her, *suddenly* (you know what that's like too I think)

"Not through, not round, what's left? I know. *Over*!

But that's impossible".

She thought again. The same. "If not round or through, it *has* to be over? Except that I can't fly".

"The swallows will help", came a whisper in her ear. WiseOwl.

Sure enough, she felt the swallows drop down the twigs they were carrying, they became strings, they became ropes, then a net to carry her up.

Kate clung on, and - up she went.

Up up up and *over*.

She looked down (was it a dream?) at the fires below. She saw they were fiercer, fiercer still, trying to reach her, burn her up. And now she was hovering over a volcano spouting fire, looking down at the molten lava licking up at her, nearly reaching her, flickering fearsome fearful fire-full fire-some burning flames.

Ohh!

And, and there to one side she saw Kris on the shore. He was looking round for her. Worried. Holly too.

She was up and over, yes. Good! But now she needed to get down.

She shut her eyes, Maybe it really *was* a dream?

Yes yes yes. She felt herself sliding, slipping, slithering down.

Ah she was there. There.

"Hullo Kris", she said opening her eyes.

But - no Kris, just the wall of flames again.

Oh oh oh, yes she'd leapt up and flown so high - but landed back on the same side again. The fires still in front of her.

The ship and Kris Kris Kris, dear friend Kris, still on the other side. Unreachable.

She sat down in despair, exhaustion.

What did she hear? A small tinkle! Sprinkle. Splatter.

Water! A little stream. Yes, a stream disappearing into the flames.

WiseOwl's voice in her ear.

"Water! water goes through flames. Just try".

"But I can't properly swim", said Kate, still terrified.

"See that big log there? Hold tight and float with it. The stream will take you safe under the flames. Hold tight".

So she did.

And there she was! Through the flames and floating now in the deep deep sea.

She knew she was saved! And that soon very soon she would find Kris, And the Pearl-Away. And her dear Holly.

But -

What was this? Why was her hand on the log feeling so hot! The *log* feeling hot! The log bursting into flames!!

Let go! *Let go!!*

Kate was floundering in the sea, nowhere else to go. The flaming log was swimming away on the horizon.

Despair.

But then -

A soft touch on her arm.

It was Holly.

"Holly, Holly, Holly", sobbed Kate, "I'm sinking, I can't swim".

Dogs can't usually smile, can they. But Holly could. She had a long rope in her mouth. "Hold onto this", she seemed to say.

So Kate held into the rope and Holly held onto Kate and - magic! There they were by the boat and Kris was pulling them both on board.

"What took you so long, Kate?" asked Kris. "Anyway I won the race didn't I".

"Um", said Kate. It was really too long a story to tell (and I think, don't you, that she didn't really want to say how afraid she'd been).

So she just pointed. There, just on the horizon, was the line of flames. As they watched it started to die down. Then only smoke. Then nothing.

"Holly saved me", she said.

So that was that.

Another good adventure.

"Bedtime", said their mum. "Till tomorrow".

Chapter 8 In the trees

Kris and Kate were walking down to the sea after their breakfast (a good bowl of porridge each, made by their mum, Kate had helped). They reached the trees at the edge of the shore that - magic - had now grown up again, only a few scorched branches left to remind them of the fire.

"WiseOwl mended them I think", whispered Kate, "or maybe it was nature's regeneration? That's magic too I think".

Kris didn't reply, he was measuring out the nearest tree with his eyes.

"I love climbing trees, don't you, Kate", he said, hooking his arm round a handy branch. Holly looked admiring but no way she was going to follow him.

"Not me", said Kate 'I'd be too frightened of falling. Look at the height of those trees!"

"I don't believe you, look it's easy", said Kris

and he pulled himself up the trunk, hand over hand right to the very very top.

Holly tried to follow. No good.

Kate didn't even try, who'd want to be up there anyway! *She* was going down to the boat. The Pearl-Away, their very own, was better than any old tree. Off she went.

Holly was torn. Who should she follow?

Ah! Kris was calling her.

"Come on Holly, come on, it's lovely up here, just one foot after another and you'll be here, easy".

"Yes of course I can", called Holly.

But for all her brave words she didn't have a clue! Dogs are wonderful, but they have wrong kind of feet for climbing trees.

Kris laughed. "Kate'll show you", he said.

But Kate was by now paddling in the sea, not helping.

"Hi Kate", shouted Kris, and his voice echoed loud under the sky and through all the trees. From high high up. "Come back, it's wonderful up here!"

He saw Kate on the shore shake her head.

"Hi Kate, come and have a look, I want to talk to you".

Kate took no notice.

"*Kate*, Holly wants you"

Kate came racing back and looked at Holly.

"*You* show me, Kate", Holly seemed to be saying.

But Kate couldn't. She sat and thought and thought.

Nothing she could do. Make a ladder?

No good. Another way?

She tried pulling with her hands.

A foot?

Another.

Oh, maybe it was easy after all.

Oh no! She'd slipped back.

Try again.

Another step.

She'd got up a little way now. Marvellous.

Oh no! she'd slipped down again.

Oh oh oh. She now couldn't move up *or* down. She was stuck. Stuck fast.

 "Oh no", she shouted, panicking, "I can't, I can't come back, come back. No good saying it's beautiful up there and that you're looking right up into the clouds, but I'm stuck, I can't go up or down, I don't know what to do, oh Kris … ".

No she wasn't going it cry, but but - well nearly (I don't blame her do you? Well, have you ever been stuck part way up a tree? Well then …).

"Come on come on" shouted Kris again, "there's a fantastic view if the Pearl-Away from up here".

"I know it's hard, very hard", came WiseOwl's whisper in Kate's ear, "but look down".

It was hard, Kate was very afraid, But she clung *hard* onto the trunk with both arms and summoned up all her bravery, and had a quick look down.

And -

and there was a snake! A snake, slithering along the ground.

And not just any snake but their friend S-Snake. He was twisting and twisting and twisting himself into a rope. A rope for Kate?

"Hold onto it with both hands", he said, "then put your feet against the tree and abseil up".

"Abseil?"

"Just do it".

So she did.

Up up up.

Up. It was easy.

"I'm here Kris", she cried in triumph, " Look".

Oh but - S-Snake had chosen the wrong tree, it was not the one Kris had climbed.

He was there - but he was on the next tree, very very high, the highest one.

Kate's was high too, but not up to his. And there was a gap, a chasm between the two.

Kate looked across at him. It was all very high up.

She looked down. Oh she hated heights, they terrified her. Could she slither down the snake-rope?

But S-Snake wasn't looking, he was just having a happy gossip about puppies and such with Holly.

"Stupid dog", said Kate, "just when I need you!" (though just what Holly could do goodness knows!).

"Come on Kate, where are you?", called Kris.

"I'm here" - just a little trembly voice from Kate.

"Where?"

" Here".

"Wh- ? Oh, I see you. Not far, that's good, just step across to my tree, easy".

Kate tried. But she couldn't reach, her arms were too short. Her legs too

"Come on, come on".

"It's too far, you'll have to come to me, then I can get a view of the Pearl-Away too".

Not easy but Kris really liked to help Kate. He reached out. Big stride with his foot. Strong boy by now, nearly a young man. Nearly.

Not quite far enough. Wobble,

He ju-u-ust managed to save himself, pull himself back to the stronger tree.

He tried again.

He caught hold of a branch near Kate to pull himself across. To her.

But it gave under his weight. He was too heavy. It broke with a hu-uge CRACK. *Broke.* Fractured.

And Kris? What happened to him when the branch he was grasping broke?

Kate heard the *bang bang bang bumping* down down down through the tree, Then an even HU-UGER CRASH onto the ground, she knew it must be Kris,

Her friend, her friend, she hadn't realised before - she depended on him, needed him, loved him for his bravery, his support, his inspiration, his love of Holly - his friendship, oh *everything*.

And he'd crashed to the ground. Must be dead. Because he'd been trying to help her because her stupid legs and arms had been too short. *Her* fault.

And she couldn't even get to him to say sorry. Or go back to tell their mum.

What was she to do?

"Oh mam, if only you were here".

A light touch on the branch as something landed next to her. It was WiseOwl, WiseOwl herself, arrived from nowhere.

"Look down", she said, "It was the sound of the *branch* falling, *not* your friend. He is safe. Look".

Kate looked down. Sure enough, there was a great branch on the ground, with Holly and S-Snake playing hide and seek around it.

Oh, and there was Kris waving from the next tree as if nothing had happened.

"Come on", he called again," come on Kate, Jump!"

"I can't, I can't". Kate was clinging on for all she was worth, "and even if I got there I wouldn't be able to hold on, it's all thorny. Spikes".

Poor Kate. I would have been scared to let go too.

"Not if you jump far enough Kate. You can see it's okay where *I* am. You'll *have* to come to me. It's not far. Easy. Just jump, I'll catch you".

"I can't , I can't, I can't".

Oh dear.

"Can't *you* come to *me*?"

"Your tree isn't strong enough for my weight. It's all right here, come on".

Kate tried again to reach. Still too far.

"I know what, Kate. Go down that tree, then climb up mine. Easy".

Good idea, Kate looked down. Oh oh, dizzying, far, imposs. And S-Snake wasn't to be seen *or* Holly.

And she was slipping. She was holding on by just one finger tip now. Slipping again.

Kris called again.

She closed her eyes. She jumped.

She felt the air slip past. Was she going down or up or east around the world? She kept her eyes fast shut in terror.

Ah she would go further than that to be with Kris.

She looked down.

There were her feet firm on a branch.

Oh, but it was that same branch where she'd been before, fingers still clutching fast to where she'd climbed.

She had *not* jumped. Not dared it after all. She'd only jumped in her *mind*. Imaginati-on.

"Come come", called Kris, Even he was wobbling now.

"I can't, I can't", she cried again, "look at the ground, too far too far".

Poor Kate.

"Go go", she hear a call, a flutter of wings, "we'll help you fly".

A flock of birds was above her, letting down small threads, strings, *ropes* from their wings for her to hold on to.

"Just shut your eyes, and you'll be there. Jump *now,* with the rope".

She did.

And she was. She did. This time she *really* did.

Aah!

She landed lightly on the branch where Kris clung, heart in his mouth a-watching her.

Would she fall, slithering down?

No, she was *there*. Wobbling, afraid, unsteady. But *there*.

With Kris.

And so she smiled, well not so much a smile as a cheeky grin. For she'd made it, she was Kate.

"I can see our ship she said. So beautiful".

"And our mam. She's waving to us".

So that was very good.

Chapter 9 The Above-The-Clouds-Land

It was wonderful up there on the tops of the trees.

"Look Kris", said Kate, " our Pearl-Away, away far far down there. What a beautiful boat she is, and what fantastic adventures we've had in her",

"Yes", said Kris. "And now for the clouds".

"What!", cried Kate.

" Our next adventure""0

"Oh oh, *more?*", thought Kate, but didn't like to say aloud, "haven't I gone through enough getting here?"

"Couldn't we just go back to the sea, to our - ", she began.

"Come on Kate", said Kris, "look at that beautiful cloud".

Kate looked. He was right. The sun was setting and the world below and around and above was flooded with iridescent gleaming rays.

"Can we reach them?" asked Kate.

"Yes", said Kris standing up on the strong branch beside her.

"Yesss", hissed the S-Snake back there down below,

"Yes", said WiseOwl's voice from - somewhere.

A distant bark from Holly.

Kate hesitated a moment.

"Yes", she said, from where she was (where else - for any of us?), "Yes".

Suddenly - there was a ladder, leading up, just a few steps, into the sky.

Kate put her foot onto the first rung and tested it for strength.

"It's all right, come on Kris", she called. "It's the way to the magic land above. Let's go".

"Yes go on, try it", came their mam's voice. "Then back home for your pancakes".

Then, suddenly -

Kate looked around. She was *there*. Somehow. She'd stepped off the ladder - oh, now she saw it was a spiral ladder - and into a new land.

Somewhere.

Above.

By the moon and in the hidden place where the north wind is born and blows and no man had trodden a mighty step before. Or a small one either.

Not just standing still or a small step either but floating through the stars of the endless eternal enduring Milky Way. By Sirius, Cassiopeia up and down and up again, dawn and sunset and evening star, and warrior Orion with his great sword.

Then through the universes' galaxies and black holes and the creation of All Things.

"It's wonderful here", whispered Kate, " but I, I want my mam. We said we'd be home for tea".

And why hadn't Kris come too?

She imagined what he'd say -

"Pancakes today?" he'd ask (he was a good boy, as you know by now, and tried to look after Kate, but, well - more interested in food than time-keeping). I suppose we could … "

Kate heard him clearly now."Well what?" said Kate crossly.

"How d'you think we'll get back, Kate? And where's Holly?"

"Well, um … ".

"Hot air balloon I suppose", he shouted. Teasing, Unbelieving.

Kate thought she heard him laugh. Oh, he *was* there! There after all, just behind her.

Ah yes, there he was, beside her now. Space suit (trust *him*! *Kate* was still just in her bare feet and pony tail). Oh and Holly too in a dog-suit.

Kris knew it was just a joke. A balloon indeed! "Silly Kate to take me seriously", he laughed cheerfully, "as usual".

But - there *was* something down there below. Floating up to them.

Wow, yes, it *was* a balloon. A large basket beneath it, Holly had somehow got into it, somewhere, and was peeping over the side at them, wagging her tail. Just waiting for them to get in.

"But - hot air", whispered Kris, "I don't think it works up here, something to do with atmosphere. Er - chemistry".

"Aeronautics", said Kate loftily. "Anyway I don't trust it".

"I do", said Kris. He stepped in.

He patted Holly.

And there he was, already piloting the balloon.

A sudden whoosh from a wind just behind them, and off the balloon went.

Went with Kris and Holly. Not with Kate.

Another whoosh. The wind whistled past as they went.

They were smaller and smaller now in the sky below.

They disappeared.

Just a little cloud now

and -

a tiny tiny Pearl-Away even further below

and -

SILENCE.

Kate was alone, alone alone alone in the universe.

Alone. By herself.

No Kris,

No Holly.

"Not alone", came the voice. WiseOwl? Herself? Her own bravery? What else could it be?

"Here too owls are wise", it said,"hold on to me, we'll fly down together".

It was her friend, yes it was, WiseOwl.

So they did.

And who do you think got there first?

"The first pancake is for you Kate, you won", said their mother.

"Oh!!" protested Kris. "Oh well, I suppose she deserves it. Anyway the next pancake's bigger, that one's mine isn't it".

"Mam mam we had such adventures up there, we … ".

"Yes yes Kate, it was great. And it was good too that you got back in good time, we'll done, now just eat up, nearly time for bed".

"Not yet … ".

"*Yes.* Look, Kris is asleep already. Holly too. And - ah - you".

Kate was asleep now too.

"Goodnight, dream of your next adventure".

Chapter 10 The next adventure

"Wake up Kate, time to get up",

"Oh oh mam" said Kate, fiercely rubbing her eyes, " I was having such an awful dream, I was … ".

"Thank goodness you woke up then, lazy head, all over now, gone, breakfast's been ready for ages".

"Kris? Is, is he all right?" Kate asked, still half in her dream. Wobbly.

"Oh yes, of course, he's gone on down …"

"Ohh! In the balloon, ohh, I remember that I … ".

"No, silly, down to the shore, says he'll see you there. Come on, you must have your porridge before you go, but I'll let you off the washing-up so you don't keep him waiting".

Kate gobbled her porridge extra quick (not very tidily, but you know what it's like when you're in a hurry, she was in a real rush to get down to Kris and the Pearl-Away),

"Bye", she called as she raced off..

She seemed to race into her dream again, more and more, further and further. She was in a balloon, in a bus, in a life jacket, swimming, not-swimming, sinking, deep in the sea, no Kris, it was washing right over her head now.

There was the ladder again, up into the clouds.

Kate put her foot onto the first rung and tested it for strength.

"It's all right, come on Kris", she called. "It's the way to another magic land. Let's go".

"Yes go on, try it", came their mum's voice. "Be brave".

Kate took a big breath and pulled Kris after her and Holly barked in excitement and scrambled up too.

And what did they find there? Another magical land!

And what was it like *this* time? Well, you'll just have to wait and see, won't you!

But you can be quite sure that when they got back they told their mam all about it as they were drying the dishes.

THE END

(for this time)

Read next

Want to know what happens next? It's in

Black pearl island

And more about the real, full, story of the adventures you've just been reading about in

Voyage of the Pearl of the Seas

And then after that in the later volumes of the Kate-Pearl series.

NOTES

You might like to know

Prologue: " ... and all that is there". The children explore magical places through their ventures, their dreams and their imagination - -as children do. This is part of adult experience too, in the magical extraordinary hidden within the ordinary things of our everyday lives (for further examples and explanation see Ruth Finnegan, *The hidden ordinary*, 2021; also other volumes in the Kate-Pearl series).

"Life is short, but life is sweet ... ": this is based on the stories of the sweet-singing golden-haired "Sirens" luring sailors to their death, told by Homer and other ancient Greek writers. The song here is the version as it appears in Charles Kingsley's *The Heroes.*

"Well, you'll just have to wait and see, won't you!" - in the next Kate-Pearl book.

The Kate-Pearl series

An engrossing series by Ruth Finnegan that takes children of all ages from cradle to - well, to anywhere

For children

Oh Kate! Your first counting book, illustrations by Rachel Backshall (0-3 years)

The Magic Adventure. Kris and Kate build a boat, a picture book, illustrations by Rachel Backshall (2-6)

Kris and Kate's next adventure. Out to the wide wide sea, a picture story book, illustrations by Abby Smith (3-8)

The Enchanted Pearl-Away, a chapter book, illustrations by Sepi (7-11)

Intermediate

Voyage of Pearl of the Seas, a fairytale prequel to "The Black Inked Pearl", illustrations by Rachel Backshall (young adult)

Black Pearl Island: Kris and Kate, children of the universe (young adult)

Adult

The Black Inked Pearl, a journey of the soul

The Helix Pearl: the tale of the wine-dark garrulous sea.

Pearl of the Wind

Fire Pearl, tale of the burning way

Pearl in the deep wood, the voice of the living trees

THE KATE-PEARL ROMANTIC SERIES

𝒫

L - #0074 - 230623 - C0 - 210/148/6 - PB - DID3613374